The Big Mog Book

Judith Kerr

Collins

An Imprint of HarperCollinsPublishers

This edition first published in Great Britain
by HarperCollins Publishers Ltd in 1997

3 5 7 9 10 8 6 4 2

ISBN: 0 00 198293-1

Printed and bound in Belgium by Proost

Contents

Mog
on
Fox
Night

One day Mog did not want to eat her supper.

It was fish. But Mog always had an egg for breakfast.

She thought, "Why shouldn't I have an egg for supper as well?"

She looked at the fish. Then she looked at Mrs Thomas.

She made a sad face. "Oh dear," said Mrs Thomas.

"Perhaps that fish isn't very nice."

"I'll give her some kitty food," said Nicky.
Mog looked at the kitty food. Then she looked at Nicky.
She made an even sadder face.

"I know," said Debbie. "She wants an egg."
Just then Mr Thomas came in from the garden.

Mr Thomas had been putting the binbags out
for the binmen to take away in the morning.
Mr Thomas did not like doing the binbags.
He liked it even less when it was snowing,
and he was cross.

He said, "You spoil that cat. That cat has
been given two suppers and has left them both.
She is not to be given an egg as well.
In fact, if that cat does not eat every bit
of those two suppers, she will not get
an egg for her breakfast either."
And he put the egg back in the fridge.

Mog was very sad when the egg went back in the fridge.
She was also very cross. She hissed at Mr Thomas.
Then she hissed at the fridge.

And then
she ran
through her
cat flap
and out into
the garden.

The garden was very cold.
There was snow everywhere.

But there was no snow under the binbags.
Mog crept under a binbag and went to sleep.

Debbie and Nicky were sad too when they went to bed.
"Mog never eats anything she doesn't like," said Debbie.
"She'll never eat that fish and the kitty food."
"And then she won't get an egg for her breakfast,"
said Nicky. "She'll be so cross."

Mog was cross even in her sleep.

She had a cross dream.
It was a dream about Mr Thomas.
Mr Thomas had put all the eggs
in the world into a binbag.
He wanted to take the binbag away.
Mog tried to stop him...

Suddenly she woke up.

There was snow all over her.

The binbag had gone.

Had Mr Thomas taken it away?

She looked.

Then she thought, this is too much.

First they give me a horrible supper,

and now there's a fox in my garden.

The fox had made a hole in the binbag

and was pulling things out of it.

What is he doing? thought Mog.

The fox ate one of the things
he had pulled out of the binbag.
It was a chicken bone.

Then he ate something else.
It was a piece of fish.
Mog knew that piece of fish.
She had left it in her dish the day before.
It had not been nice then.
She thought, that fox is mad.

Then she saw something else.

The fox had a little fox.

No, he had two little foxes.

He was giving them bits to eat

out of the binbag.

But one of the little foxes
only wanted to play.

It played with the snow.

It played
with a twig.

It played with
an old tin.

And then it wanted to play with Mog.

Mog thought, I don't want to play with that
little fox, and she ran through her cat flap
and back into the house.

But the little fox ran after her.

And the other little fox ran after the first little fox.

And the big fox ran after them both.

Mog thought, this is really too much.
First they give me a horrible supper.
Then there's a fox in my garden,
and now there are three foxes in my kitchen.

The foxes liked Mog's kitchen.

They liked the sink.

They liked the pots and pans.

They
liked
the
kitchen
cupboard,

and the breakfast table and Mog's basket.
Mog thought, there are too many foxes here.
I'm going!

She found a much nicer
place and went to sleep.

Very early in the morning she woke up.
Debbie woke up too.

Debbie said, "Look who's in my bed.
Why aren't you in your basket, Mog?"
Nicky said, "I wonder if she's eaten her supper."

They went down to the kitchen to see.
Mog's two dishes were empty.
"She's eaten it!" said Nicky.

Then they saw something else.

"I don't think it was Mog who ate it," said Debbie.

The foxes thought it was time to go home.
They ran out through the cat flap.

Then they ran off through the garden.

It had stopped snowing and it was a lovely day.

Debbie and Nicky
tidied the kitchen.

They tidied up every bit.

"Now you can go back in
your basket, Mog," said Nicky.
Just then Mr and Mrs Thomas came in.
Mr Thomas looked at the empty dishes.
"There," he said. "What a good cat.
I knew Mog would eat her supper in the end."

Debbie and Nicky said nothing.
After all, they thought, no one really
knew *who* had eaten Mog's supper.

Mog had

a lovely egg

for her breakfast.

She was very pleased.

And the foxes were pleased too.

For Lucy and Alexander

Mog
and
Bunny

One day Mog got a present.
"Here you are, Mog," said Nicky.
"This is for you. It's called Bunny."

Mog liked Bunny.

She carried him about.

She played with him . . .

and played with him . . .

and played . . .

and played . . .

and played with him.

He was her best thing.

When Mog came to have her supper,
Bunny came too.

Sometimes Mog thought
Bunny would like a drink.

But Bunny wasn't very good at drinking.
"Oh dear," said Debbie. "Look where Bunny's got to."

And she put him on the radiator to dry.

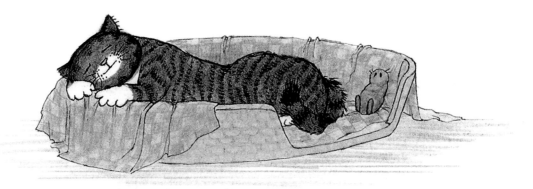

At night Bunny slept with Mog in her basket.

During the day, when Mog was busy,
she always put Bunny somewhere nice.
You never knew where Bunny would get to.

Sometimes Bunny liked to be quiet and cosy,

and sometimes he liked to be where there was a lot going on.

Mr and Mrs Thomas didn't understand this.
They didn't say, "Look where Bunny's got to."
They shouted, "Yukk!"

They yelled, "Arrgh! What a horrible, dirty thing!"

And they threatened
to throw Bunny away
in the dustbin.

One day Mr Thomas said,
"Let's have supper in the garden."

Everyone helped to carry things out of the house.

It was a lovely supper.

But suddenly . . .

. . . there was a crash of thunder and it poured with rain.

"Quick! Inside!" shouted Mrs Thomas. "It's bedtime anyway."

"Where's Mog?"
said Debbie.
"I expect she's keeping
dry under a bush,"
said Mrs Thomas.
"She'll come in later."

In the middle of the night,
Debbie and Nicky
woke up. Mog
hadn't come
in and it was
still pouring
with rain.

"Let's go and find her," said Debbie.

It was very dark in the garden.
They shouted, "Mog! Where are you, Mog?"
But nothing happened.

Then they heard a meow.
"There she is!" shouted
Nicky. "Come on Mog!
Come inside!"
But Mog just went
on sitting in
the rain.

It was . . .

dripping . . .

off her nose.

"What's the matter, Mog?" said Debbie.
Then she said, "Oh dear! Look where Bunny's got to!"

Nicky picked Bunny
up and showed him
to Mog.
"It's all right, Mog,"
he said. "We've set
Bunny free. You can
come inside now."

Then they carried Bunny through the dark garden . . .

and through the house . . .

and they put him on the radiator to dry.

Then they all had a big sleep.

In the morning they told Mrs Thomas
what had happened, and how Mog had
stayed with Bunny in the dark and the rain.

Debbie said, "You won't really throw
Bunny away in the dustbin, will you?"
Mrs Thomas said, "No, never. It would
make Mog too sad."

Then she sighed and said, "Perhaps he's not quite
so horrible, now he's been washed by the rain."
They all looked on the radiator.

But this is where Bunny had got to.

For Eve and Thomas
and their Granny and Grandpa

Mog
and the
Granny

One day Mog was waiting for Debbie
to come home from school.
Mog always knew when Debbie was coming.
She didn't know how she knew. She just knew.
Suddenly a picture would come into her head
of Debbie coming down the road.
Then she would go to meet her.
Debbie said, "School's all finished for
the summer, Mog. Isn't it exciting!"
Mog said nothing. She didn't like things
to be exciting. She liked them to be the same.

Inside the house
everyone was excited too.
Mrs Thomas was packing.

Mr Thomas
was looking
for something
important.

Nicky was dancing
and singing a song
he had made up.

"We're going to America where the skyscrapers are.
We're not going by train but on an aeroplane.
We'll see all the sights,
and it will be very
surprising because
they have their
days when we
have our
nights!"

Debbie said, "You can't come, Mog.
But you're going to a nice granny's house.
She'll look after you till we come back."

Next day Mog went to the granny's house.

The granny was old with very thin legs.

First Mog thought she had three legs.

Then she saw that one of them was a stick.

Debbie said, "Goodbye, dear Mog."

The granny said, "I'll look after Mog.

And she'll have my Tibbles for company."

Mog thought, "Tibbles? Nobody told me

that there would be another cat.

At least he sounds quite small."

Tibbles had been small to start with but then he had grown. "Here's a little friend for you," said the granny.

Tibbles liked surprising people.

And he liked Mog's basket. The granny said, "Don't be silly, Tibbles. Let Mog have her basket, and you can sleep on my bed."

Mog sat in her basket, but she couldn't sleep.
She thought of her house. She thought of Debbie.
Suddenly a picture of Debbie came into her head.
Debbie was in a high place and there were even
higher places all round. It was all too high.
Mog didn't think Debbie should be there.

"Whatever is the matter, Mog?" said the granny.

"You'd better come and snuggle up with us."

A few days later the postman brought a card.

"It's from Debbie," said the granny.

"She's been to the top of a skyscraper."

Mog thought the card smelled of Debbie.

Tibbles didn't have a card.

He had tea in a saucer instead.

He was very fond of tea.

Tibbles had an open window instead of a cat flap.
He had a yard to play in.

Sometimes Mog and Tibbles played together.

Sometimes they chased each other.

Sometimes they liked each other

and sometimes they didn't.

The granny gave them nice food to eat.
She went to the shops to buy it.
They always had the same, but they
always thought the other one's was nicer.

The first time the granny went shopping, Mog had a big surprise.
The granny no longer had a stick. She had wheels instead.

She gave Tibbles a ride.

"What about you, Mog?" said the granny.
But Mog thought the wheels were too surprising.

One day the granny put out her best tea cups.
She said, "We're going to have a party."
It was very hot, so they had the party in the yard.

A lot of other grannies came. They were surprised to see Mog.
The granny told them about Mog's people. She said,
"They've been all over America and now they're ending up
at a special Red Indian show."

The grannies stayed a long time.
Mog got very tired.
She thought of Debbie and
she wondered what Red Indians were.

Suddenly a picture of Debbie came into her head.

Debbie was smiling at a big bird.

Mog knew it was a bird because it had feathers.

But it had a face like a person. It was a person bird.

And there were more person birds nearby.

Why was Debbie smiling? Those big person birds

might fly away with her and hurt her.

Mog wanted to save Debbie.
She did a big jump.
Tibbles liked tea inside him, not outside.
"Oh dear," said the granny.

"Oh dear," said all the other grannies.

"And your best cup too." Then they went home.

That night Mog did not
sleep in the granny's bed.
She was too sad.

She was still sad in the morning.
She thought of Tibbles and
the granny being upset.
She thought of Debbie
and the person birds.

Suddenly a picture of Debbie came into her head.
The person birds had not hurt her at all.
Instead they had given her some of their feathers
and a baby person bird as a present. She was
smiling and excited, and she was coming home.
Mog thought, "I must be there to meet her."

She ran out of the yard

and across a road

and down another road

...and up a tree.

After a time the dog went home.
Mog wanted to go home too,
but she couldn't get down the tree.

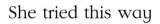 She tried this way

 and that way,

but she was stuck,
and it was getting late,
and Debbie would
be coming home.

Mog thought, "There's nobody to help me."
But there was somebody.

"Quick, Mog! Jump!" said the granny,
and Mog jumped.

"We'll have to get a move on," said the granny.

"We haven't much time," said the granny.

104

"I think we can just make it," said the granny.

AND THEY DID!

When Debbie got home, Mog was there to meet her.

"We've never had such excitement," said the granny.
"Mog will have to come and stay with Tibbles again."

Mog said nothing.

She didn't like things to be exciting.

She liked them to be the same.